EXPEDITION HOME PARTI

Expedition home part1

zuri island

papa s. and Renee Gudex

yucky papa ink

1

Expedition Home Part 1: Zuri Island
BY
Papa s. and Renee Gudex

Sam sat in his easy chair drinking coffee and watching the news. On the news another law that would have protected freedom of religion got shot down. Now strife and riots all over the world. Once again Russia trying to bring another democratic republic under their communist thumb. The FCC threatening to take devices away from TV and radio stations airing news that put bad light on president and his administration.

The news anchor said the clip coming up is the attorney general.

"The president has asked me to make the announcement that the law of 1865 that was passed to reconstruct the south after the civil will be enforced as of today."

The anchor came back on and said, we investigated the law and found that it means if you discriminate against a minority, that they can claim your property as their own.

She then said, "there's more" and she played the clip.

The attorney general went on to say "the president has signed an executive order that any immigrant who voluntarily joins the presidents newly formed fed police force will be given immediate citizenship.

The anchor came back on. "Both republicans and democrats are stating the order is illegal and unconstitutional."

Sam knew this was not good. He got out of his chair turned off the TV and went to the bank. He withdrew all the money in his account.

The clerk asked, "is there a problem?"

"No, I am making a large investment."

As Sam walked out of the bank. An almost panic-stricken crowd began filling up the bank fast. Sam drove home he turned on the radio.

> "the speaker of the house called the president to discuss the issue and was told the president was too busy to talk to him. If he needed to talk to the president, he could make an appointment for next week and the man hung up the phone.

> The speaker of the house called an emergency meeting of the house. The senior member of the senate did the same. When the legislators approached the capital building, they were stopped by armed guards, and told the capital building was closed until further notice. if they knew what is good for them, they would leave and have no future gatherings without a permit.

> The federal legislators have contacted their state governors. As they talked to the governors, armed guards approached them and demanded their cell phones be surrendered. if they refused, they would be arrested. Those who protested were arrested. The rest of them immediately surrendered their cell phones and disbursed."

Suddenly the radio went dead.

Sam called his brother, "if you have any money then I suggest you go and get all of it out now and hurry!"

"Why?"

"Just do it! I'll explain later trust me."

"We don't understand?"

"Turn on your TV or radio and tell me what you see or hear?" After a short time, Terry replied "They aren't transmitting."

"I know. Now get to your bank and get your money out."

Sam pulled into a coffee shop parking lot and went into the shop. He ordered coffee and ice water.

The waitress said, "cash only, credit and debit cards won't be accepted."

"Ok, why? what's going on?"

"I don't know," said the waitress, "The banks aren't accepting card charges at this time. You got cash?"

"Yes," said Sam," how much is coffee today?"

"$12 a cup."

"I'll pass," said Sam as he walked out of the restaurant.

As Sam got into his car a police car drove by. A loudspeaker announced, "marshal law has been declared by the president. Anybody out after dark will be arrested. "

Sam looked at his gas gauge. He knew if coffee is $12 a cup gas is out of sight. Sam looked at his gas gauge again and it was three quarters full. As Sam drove, he saw a gas station, the sign said, gas purchase by appointment only, call twenty-four hours ahead.

Growing even more concerned Sam called Terry again. "Hi, did you go to the bank?"

"Yes," said his brother, "we took out all our money. So, what is going on? I heard on the news the president shut down the house and senate." Said Terry.

"A coffee shop said banks aren't accepting card charges, and I saw a gas station sign requiring appointments to buy gas. The president has declared martial law and a dusk curfew."

Sam's family said "we work nights. Are we supposed to go to work or what?"

"I don't know" said Sam, "I suggest you call your boss."

Sam hung up as he pulled into the driveway his radio came back on.

> "The government announced ration cards will be issued to all citizens. You must have a ration card for anything you purchase. No ration card, no rations. All rations will be issued from 8AM to 5PM on a first come first serve basis. If you do not get your rations by 5 PM that day, you must come back the next day. Anyone caught dealing in or with the black market will be shot on the spot. Their family's ration card will be revoked. Anyone caught in the act of a crime will be shot on sight. Anyone suspected of committing a crime will be shot on sight. Anyone participating in a rebellious act or open rebellion will be shot on sight. Anyone without a government ID card will be shot on sight. Anyone on the streets after dark without a government pass will be shot on sight. All guns held by known military persons must be turned in to the government within the next 48 hours. Those not complying will be shot on sight. No one may travel out of the district they live in without a pass. Those caught doing so will be shot on sight."

5 years later Sam and his brother Terry had learned to adapt in new not so united states and had even managed to use what money and skills they had to help others escape the oppressive government. Now run by a group of pseudo scientists claiming to be doctors. There job was to use fear and government propaganda to fuel the socialist government and use fear and shame to keep the population from asking questions...

The year was 2025, John and his wife sat by his mother's hospital bed. Only 95 years young and dying. A hospital administrator came into the room. His eyes were cold his and his voice was even colder.

"Under the law passed recently dying patients have to be discharged after 5 days. If he could not care for her, she would be sent to a place that could. Say your final farewells to your mother. Other than the hospital bill there will be no charge to you. Now sign this paper and don't forget to take her belongings before you leave."

With that he left the room. John and his wife held hands and prayed for his mother. John started to cry. John's wife gathered her mother in laws belongings. As John and his wife left the room, he read his copy of the paper he signed.

"stop at the checkout office."

John went to the office as his wife took his mother's belongings to the car. Inside the office a sign read:

"take a number and have a seat".

There were 45 people in the waiting room. Every few minutes a number was called and one of the people would go up to the counter. Five women worked behind the counter. When the people walked away from the counter, they were sad and sometimes crying. As fast as a number was called, more people came into the office. After 2 ½ hours John's number was called. He walked up to the counter a tall slender woman spoke. Her voice as cold as the administrators:

"papers"

Quietly handed them to her without a sound, still trying to process what was happening.

"Did you get all of the deceased's belongings out of the room."

Rage and confusion began to boil up inside of him, but knew it was pointless to make a scene. After all, 90 % of the hospitals around these days were nothing but legal extortion rings.

"When I left, she was still alive, but yes we did as you asked"

The women rolled her eyes and spoke in a sharp annoyed voice as though the simple action of having to do the job that she was so generously being paid for was so difficult.

"Sign this"

He did and she gave him a death certificate.

"She's still alive" He all but yelled at her.

The woman ignored him and called the next number. John stood there the rage and confusion inside him growing even stronger.

"Sir either move or I'll call security."

He stared the nurse straight in the eye. A stare so dark if looks could kill she would have been dead on the spot.

"Yes ma'am" bitter sarcasm dripping in his voice.

When John got home, he called his attorney.

"I'm sorry john but with the new law, terminally ill patients can only be in the hospital for 5 days. After that, the next of kin have the option of letting the government deal with the patient or the next of kin can take them home. Basically, john the government euthanized your mom."

"What about her body? Can't I even give her a decent burial"

The lawyer said, "it's a government secret. No one knows. I have heard they are recycled. How or where I do not know. If I were you, I wouldn't go trying to find out."

John thanked the lawyer and hung up.

With tears in his eyes he told his wife what the lawyer said. John called his job and told them his mother had died and he needed some time off

"You get 1 day. The day she died and that's it. Any more than that will be cause for dismissal."

John was totally outraged and beside himself. John's wife handed him a drink. He could see the love and warmth in her eyes.

"Here, you look like you need it."

A few days later the power bill came. It read $75 taken from the bank and a $75 credit. Confused John asked his wife if she overpaid the bill last time.

"Not to my knowledge"

John checked his bank statement the right amount was taken out last month. John called the power company and a recording said

"if your bill is lower than normal you've received a recycle credit. To speak to a representative push zero. Leave your name and phone number and you will be contacted within 48 hours. There is a $5 service charge for the return call. "

John said a few choice but colorful words as he hung up the phone without leaving a message. After a few days passed, when John came home from work, his wife handed him a letter that came in the mail that day. It was from the government. He sat and opened the letter and read it.

"your mother's estate was $48,300 minus 50% redistribution tax, $20,000 hospital bill and $2,000 income tax the remaining balance is $2,300. Please accept our condolences."

In a terribly angry voice, John went into a rant using very colorful language. Knowing his anger was not directed at her but at the situation his wife listened with compassion and understanding.

"where does it end. How many times must we get ripped off?"

"Let me see the letter and the check"

John gave it to her. Through his head in his hands in defeat.

She looked at it closely Hoping she could find some silver lining. Unfortunately, there was only darker news. Softly she spoke.

"Did you see where you only have ten business days to cash the check or you will forfeit the funds."

Still outraged, he said, "let me that. This is unbelievable." Shaking his head and muttering under his breath. John made a drink and went and sat on his front porch to drink it. john's neighbor, Frank passed by shortly after.

"You look upset."

"Upset doesn't begin to describe how I feel" and he went on to tell Frank what happened. After he finished telling his story.

the neighbor gave him his sympathies then said, "you can't do much about it but does suck. The same happened to me and I had to pay $5,000 to the hospital. "

After sitting a few moments in silence frank speaking quieter then he had before questioned:

"Am I safe in assuming you're not government secret officer?"

"Yes," said John." Why?"

"My wife's brother can help people escape the country for a fee if you are interested" said Frank.

"Hang loose" said John

"come out here baby."

His wife came out.

John looked her in the eye and spoke "listen up, tell my wife what you told me and please elaborate."

Frank began "My wife's brother makes a living helping people escape the country for a fee of $500 a head. He set up things with a fishing boat owner who charges $2,000 a head."

John's wife asked. "How do you know you can trust these people?"

"I trust my brother in law enough that me and my wife are going to do it" said Frank.

John and his wife looked at each other as if to silently consult each other.

"we'll do it" They both replied in unison

"What do we have to do?" He asked Frank.

"Because of government laws you can only take small amounts of money out of the bank at a time. unless you provide a contract for purchase and then you must leave 15% in the bank. Every two to three weeks they make a few more tries to an island nation called Zuri"

"It's a republic with low taxes, they help tradesmen, doctors, and engineers like you and me set up housekeeping and find employment. In some cases, they pay a bonus" explained Frank.

"However, government patrol boats patrol the waters. You will have to pose as a fishing boat crew in case the boat is stopped by a patrol boat."

"How much are taxes there," asked John?

"It's 15% flat income tax and 2% medical care tax per family and no sales tax." Answered Frank.

"That beats the heck out of a 50% redistribution tax plus income tax," said John.

"What do we do first," asked John's wife?

"First how much money do you have in the bank minus 15%?" asked Frank.

John and his wife got their bank app and calculated 85%.

"We figure $98,000" stated John.

"OK" said Frank," do not act any different than normal. I'll get a contract from my brother in law, give it to you, you go to the bank, take out the money, give me $500 a head, I'll give the $1,000 to my brother in law and get instructions for the next step from him."

Frank then breathed in deeply and looked john seriously in the eye. His voice now growing even quieter.

"Do not! I repeat! do not! speak to anyone including your friends or your relatives about what you're doing. Your freedom and life depend on absolute secrecy"

Frank's wife came and joined them. John got four more drinks for the four of them.

They finished their drinks.

Frank said, "Do not sell or give away any belongings and be sure to make all your payments on your accounts just like always to avoid any suspicion. I will have the contract you'll need for your bank in two or three days. Do not talk about this to anyone including yourselves in case somebody might overhear you."

With that, Frank and his wife said goodbye and went home.

John and his wife went into the house. his wife asked if he was hungry.

"You know all of a sudden, I could eat a horse," he said.

"I feel a lot better too", she said.

As she made dinner, she and John exchanged pleasant thoughts about their future being careful not to speak of their trip or when.

As the next two days passed, John and his wife saw little of Frank and wife. John's wife asked him if possibly they had been ripped off for the money, they gave the neighbors.

"I don't think so," said John. "It's best we do not talk about it for now. Let us go to bed and relieve some tension."

His wife sighed concern still written on her face "perhaps your right." She followed him to bed praying to god her husband's instincts were correct.

The next morning, John was awakened by the doorbell. He put on his PJ's and answered the door. It was Frank.

"Good morning neighbor. Any chance of getting a cup of coffee?"

"Sure thing, come on in. I will get the wife up. She will make some fresh."

When John came back in the room Frank was holding some legal-size papers.

"Is that what I think it is?" John questioned sternly.

"Yes," said Frank, "Can I use your cell phone?"

Frank took the phone from John and put it under the couch cushion. When John's wife came into the room, he did the same with hers as well as his own.

"How about some music?" suggested Frank with a twinkle of mischief in his eye.

John turned on the stereo. Frank gestured with his hands to turn up the volume.

"Come sit close. Now It is safe to talk," said Frank as he handed John a copy of the contract. "Take this to your bank and draw out the $98,000 in cash. After that go to the address on the contract and ask for a woman named Gloria. If a man there says Gloria passed on, give him the contract. He will tell you what to do next. Be sure and take the $98,000.00 with you. Also take your driver's license, bank cards and birth certificates. Leave all other government ID's and club membership cards here. Take only the clothes on your back and a light jacket. After your done getting the money at the bank, discard your driver's licenses and bank cards in the nearest trash can outside of the bank. When you leave here if it does not fit in your purse or pocket leave it here."

John and his wife still processing the information frank had just given them merely nodded.

"One more thing, do not! I repeat, do not take your phones' or pills of any kind! They have ways of finding people who have those things on them. All you should have on you when we go to the business is a birth certificate, cash and two pictures, one of man and one of woman and that is all. Any questions?

"Can I take my jewelry?" asked John's wife.

"No," said Frank, "only your birth certificate, the pictures and cash only. Do not even wear wedding rings. My wife will be here shortly. You may want to take your morning shower before we leave. Leave everything here to look like you are coming back. We can all go in the same car. We should leave within the hour."

Frank took a drink of coffee, "once we walk out of the house, don't speak of what we're doing until we get to the business and then only when necessary."

"You will need to get your hair cut like a man's," Frank told John's wife. "Do that as soon as possible. Also, all of us will take a laxative in the event any pills were taken in the last 48 hours to eliminate them from our bodies. The women will have to wear their breasts with elastic bandages, so they don't show. The idea is to look like a man. Do not wear any makeup, none whatsoever. We all will wear a man's white tee shirt, no bra and jeans and deck shoes."

They all took a fast-acting laxative in ten-minute increments. John and his wife took a shower, got dressed and got rid of all their government ID's and documents. Keeping only bank cards, birth certificates and driver's licenses like Frank told them.

The four of them got in the car and drove to the bank. On the way to the bank, Jon and his wife were nervous. Frank told them, "smile be of good cheer, it's a beautiful sunny day, right?"

"Right," they said as they smiled and tried to be calm.

When they got to the bank, they all got out of the car and walked toward the bank door.

As they did, Frank said, "don't say any more than necessary while in the bank. Also, stay calm and smile."

Everything went smooth and quick in the bank. The teller asked, "do you want cash or a check?" Both Frank and John said, "cash please."

After the teller handed them the money he said, "Take care your carrying a lot of money and good luck to you. Have a nice day."

All four of them said thank you and left the bank. When they got outside, John's wife said, "I feel like I just took a big dump after being constipated for a week." They all agreed and laughed.

There is a trash can, said John. All of them threw their ID's and bank cards in the can and walked to the car.

They drove to the business.

When they arrived, they parked in a nearby grocery store lot. They all got out of the car careful not to look suspicious.

"you all know what to do?" Frank asked quietly.

"yes" the other 3 answered.

"Good, Lets do this." A look of determination crossing his face.

They walked into the business. The sign said: **commercial properties sold here**. There were two men in the office.

One of the men rose from his seat and shook all four of their hands. "Have a seat, I'll be with you shortly." He said pointing to a row of chairs. The two men shook hands and one left. John quietly said to Frank, "this doesn't' feel right."

"Relax" replied Frank. Still staring forward his face stoic to hide his nervousness.

After the man filed some papers, he said, "Can I help you fclks?"

Frank replied, "we're here to see Gloria."

The man said, "Gloria passed away. will you please come into my private office?"

They followed the man into his office.

"Have a seat make yourselves comfortable," the man said. "Do you have any ID's?"

"no, we have birth certificates."

"Can I see them?"

They all handed him their certificates.

"Do you have pictures to show me?" He asked

The women gave him their pictures. The man looked at the pictures. "Do you have a contract with Gloria?" he asked.

The men handed the man their contracts. He looked over the documents and gave them back the birth certificates.

"I did some calculations and wrote down a set of figures for each couple. "

John and Frank each looked at their papers each showed $4,000 for their membership.

He then said, "Give me all but $300 of your money. I will explain why in a few minutes." John went first, the man counted the money. He told John, "With the current rate of exchange, minus my fee, you get back $82,000.00. If you agree, we go to the next step."

John said "ok." he knew he did not have a choice. The man counted out $82,000.00 in Zuri currency and handed it to John. John and he then shook hands as though to solidify their deal. Frank went next. After he finished with Frank the man said, "Listen very carefully and do everything I say and by tomorrow you will be in Zuri. OK?"

"Ok" they said. He gave the women some medical tape and said "Take $5 in singles from the new currency and tape the rest to your waste. Do it now." The man shredded the pictures and contracts. While the women secured the money to their bodies, he told Frank and John the next step. He asked, "where did you park your car?"

John replied, "In the food store lot."

"Very good" said the man. He went on, "At this point, all you should have on you is $300 government currency, new currency, and a birth certificate. Is that the case?"

Frank said, "we still have car keys, wallets, purses, and jackets."

"Follow me."

The four of them followed the man to the outer office. "Do you see the bus tour office across the street?"

"yes".

"Go to the office and buy four tickets for the fishing pier tour. Use the government currency you kept, not the new currency. After you have bought the tour tickets go outside. Discard any remaining government documents, currency, all keys, purses, and wallets. At that all you should have is Zuri currency and birth certificates. Each couple should have some dollars of the new money in your pocket. That is your pass for the boat. Carry your jackets it is too warm outside to wear them. After you discard everything, except the new money, tour tickets, and birth certificates, go back into the tour office and wait until told to board the bus. When you get to the fishing piers, get off by the anchor bar. Walk to the piers. Look for a boat named Glorias Crossing. Ask the man standing on the deck "Permission to board?" After he says yes, go on board. He will ask you for change for a ten. Give him the ten singles in new currency and tell him "my condolences for Gloria passing.""

"Got it" said the man?

"Got it" they all replied in unison.

The man shook their hands. "Good luck!"

The two men and their wives crossed the street and went into the tour office. They bought their tickets and asked when the next tour was. The ticket agent replied, "Tours every hour."

John's wife asked if she had a brochure on the tour.

The agent handed her a brochure. "Enjoy the tour."

John's wife thanked her. She found John and the others outside of the tour office. She gave the others their tickets and kept one for herself. "It seems a waste to throw away $200 cash" said John.

"Let's see it," said Frank. John gave him the old currency. "Frank added his money to it and threw it in the trash can along with keys, wallets and purses."

"Your turn John."

He did likewise.

"Frank let's take quiet but quick inventory: BC, Tour tickets, and $10 singles NC."

After the four checked their pockets, one at a time each said, "I'm good."

They went back in the tour office and waited for the bus to load. The four talked small talk laughing, being careful not to create any suspicion or any unwanted attention. The agent announced the fishing tour boat was now loading. The four went to the tour bust showed the driver their tickets and took a seat on the bus.

A woman got on the bus the door closed and the woman spoke into a microphone.

Welcome to fisherman pier tours. From time to time I will point out attractions along the way. If you have any questions, please don't hesitate to ask.

As the bus passed different attractions the guide told his story.

The guide talked about the statue of liberty.

"That's something isn't it?" remarked Frank's wife. "Somehow it doesn't mean what it did ten or fifteen years ago."

"Very true" replied the others softly. The bus came to the Anchor bar bus stop.

The Guide said, "We will stop here for one hour to get refreshments and lunch. When ordering your selection, show your ticket to get a discount and faster service. Please wait until the bus comes to a complete stop before leaving your seat."

The two men and their wives waited until all the other passengers got off the bus then got off themselves. After getting off the bus, they hung back until they were alone at the bus stop. John took a deep breath and said, "here goes nothing."

At that they walked down to the pier looking for the Glorias Crossing boat.

They were surprised how big the boat was. It had a black deck, a white hull with the name Glorias Crossing painted in big black letters on the hull. There was a large beard by the gangway. A cigarette hanging from his mouth as he leisurely read the newspaper.

"Ahoy" said Frank loudly, "Permission to board?"

The Man look up from his newspaper, as if startled someone had disturbed his peace and quiet. A look of annoyance flashed his faced.

"Permission granted." He replied in deep gravelly voice.

They walked up the gangway to the quarter deck to the man and said, "Our condolences for Gloria's passing."

"Thank you," said the man. "Do you have change for a ten-dollar bill?"

Frank said yes. Then John and Frank took the five singles they each had in their pockets and showed the man.

"Thank you," said the man, he asked them to walk to Officer of the Day desk with him.

"Each of you write your first name and last name right her in this page and follow me."

They followed him below to the crew's mess deck.

"Have a seat and relax. The first mate will be with you shortly." He left.

Time seemed to stand still. An older man came in.

"Good afternoon, Can I please see your ID's."

They looked at each other confused. "All we have are birth certificates and new currency they replied."

"I'm the first mate if you want some coffee help yourself. God willing, and the weather holds we will be Zuri in about five or six hours. If we are stopped by a patrol boat, you will go to the crew's quarters. Get in a bunk and act like your sleeping. If boarded, we will come down from topside. Stay off the main deck until we reach our destination. Any questions?"

All four shook their heads no unsure of their own voices.

"The evening meal is at 18:00 or six PM." The first mate showed them the crews quarters, head, and went topside. The four went back to the crews mess deck and got some coffee and talked quietly between themselves. As they sat there, time seemed to stand still. After a time, they felt the boat moving. They felt a feeling of relief leaving the harbor. A short while later an older large woman came on the mess deck.

"Hi, I'm called Cookie. I'm the ships cook. Can I assume you folks will be joining us for dinner?"

They replied, "yes."

"Dinner will be about one hour from now. Do either of you know how to cook?"

Both women nodded.

"Follow me to the Galley Ladies." She stated turning to leave the room. Abruptly stopping a look on her face as though she forgot something.

"OH! Gentleman, if you would put 10 settings on the table. A dinner plate, a soup bowl, a coffee cup, a fork, knife, and spoon at each setting. Please" A slight accent coming through.

"After the meal you four can do the dishes. Understood?"

"OK" replied the four.

After dinner and the cleanup was done, Cookie told them the first mate wanted to see them on the main deck.

When they got to the main deck, they walked up to the first mate.

"Good evening sir," they said.

"Good evening," he replied.

"We are in open sea. Feel free to move about the deck. keep out of the way of the crew and keep your wits about you. If you hear three bells, be quiet and go below to the mess deck immediately. Understand?

"Yes sir," they replied.

After the first mate left, they stood by the deck rail talking. It was a warm night. The sky was full of stars. A stout man with a long beard and mustache walked up to them.

"I'm the captain and you are?" He said.

"We are going to Zuri thanks to you and your crew, thank you for that."

The captain asked to see their ID's.

"We don't have any" they replied, "All we have is our birth certificates."

"You folks enjoy the trip. We should reach our destination in about three hours" and he walked away.

Suddenly they heard three bells and went below to the mess deck. The four sat at the table.

Each wondered what was happening, but each was too concerned with their own nerves to ask.

Fearing the worst, they sat not speaking. finally, one of the wives spoke. Her voice soft almost inaudible.

"I'm scared stiff."

"We all are," snapped John," pull yourself together and be quiet."

The boat came to a stop.

After a few minutes, a crew member came to the mess deck and told the men to come with him on the double. The men followed the crew man to the main deck.

"Stand by and be quiet."

As Frank and John stood on the deck, they saw a patrol boat tied to the fishing boat. The first mate came out of the captain's cabin. He pointed at John and said, "come with me."

He ordered another man to do the same. The three men boarded the patrol boat and went below deck to the crew's quarters. There was an extremely sick man in a bunk. The first mate walked up to the bunk and took out a long sharp knife and cut the man's throat, "That should end his illness." He wiped the blood off the knife on the bunk sheets.

John was horrified. He did all he could do to keep from throwing up.

As the first mate put his knife away, he looked John square in the eye. "Pull yourself together and follow me." John did, too afraid to disagree. He told the other man to take anything of value except government money and bring it back to the boat.

"Yes sir," said the crewman.

The first mate and John went back on board the fishing boat.

The first mate told Frank and John and the crew to follow him into the captain's cabin. Inside the cabin Frank and John saw five bodies on the floor. The first mate ordered the men to carry the bodies on to the patrol boat.

"Put them below deck and make sure the hatch is closed. Joe and Mika stay on board and secure the boat. The rest of you return to the fishing boat."

Frank and John stood on the deck of the boat afraid to speak.

The first mate walked up to them. "We do what we have to do to survive. What did you see?" Frank and John both stuttered shaking their heads back and forth rapidly. "Not a damn thing!"

"Good answers" replied the first mate, "Now go below to the mess deck. I am sure the women are worried. Assure them everything is fine. we should reach Zuri in a couple of hours."

The boat started to move as the men went down a ladder to the mess deck. When the men entered the room, the women were sitting close to each other holding hands with worried, scared looks on their faces. When the women saw the men, they ran to them and hugged each other excitedly.

Both Women began to rapidly fire questions to John and Frank all at once. "what is happening? What is going on? Are we in danger?"

"Relax everything is okay. We should be in Zuri in about two hours. As far as what happened the less you know the better. However, I will say you do not want to make the men on this boat angry. Beyond that we do not know, nor did we see a damn thing.

"What's that supposed to mean?" asked the women.

"Just be glad they're on our side."

After an hour or so past the captain came on the mess deck.

"Good evening sir" said the two men.

"Good evening. How are you folks getting along?"

"We are good" they all replied cautiously.

"We should be able to see the Zuri Harbor lights very soon. If you want to you folks can come to the main deck and enjoy the view and fresh air. Just stay out of the crew's way."

"Thank you sir," said the four of them.

After that captain quietly got his coffee and left for the main deck.

The night air was warm with a gentle breeze. the sky was filled with stars. As they stood by the rail enjoying the evening and having a relaxing conversation, they heard a man yell.

"Land Ho!"

"I don't see it." They said to one another.

"We need to be on the other side of the boat," stated John. They all went to the other side.

"There they are. I see them," said Frank's wife.

"That will soon be our new home soon" stated John.

The closer the boat came to shore the more excited they got.

"I can see the dock!" John's wife said with excitement.

As the boat reached the dock the first mate told them, "we have arrived don't leave the boat until told to do so."

"Yes sir," they replied.

About 20 Minutes later the boat had finished docking and First mate approached them again.

"The captain wants to see you in his cabin, if you'll follow me please."

The four quietly obeyed.

After entering the cabin, the first mate said "Have a seat. The captain will be with you shortly. Would any of you like a beverage?"

"Thank you no," they said.

"Relax the hard part is over." said the first mate.

The men remembered what happened to the patrol crew. They each drew their wives closer just in case any issues arose.

Shortly after that the captain came in.

"Well, we are here!" The captain stated a friendly smile crossing his face for the first time sense they boarded the ship. "Before you go ashore, we want to cover a few things you need to know. If you have any questions save them until we are done okay?"

"Okay" they replied.

"Before we begin do you have a few singles for a $10 bill?"

The men replied "yes." They each took the new currency out and handed it to the captain.

The captain and examined it good and said welcome to your new country and gave them back the money.

"you will spend the rest of the night on the boat. In the morning you will go to the inauguration Center. There you will get a complete physical and initiation. You will stay there until your lab work comes back and about five or six hours. If all is good, you each will get government IDs. Then you will go to the federal bank of Zuri. There you will deposit your money and get a bankcard. I suggest keeping some cash to save for meals and such for at least two days. After that you will go to any one of the four hotels. They rent by the week. You should be able to use your bankcard for that. After that go to the national work office, they will help you find work and verify any licenses or education requirements you have. I suggest you purchase a cell phone so employers can contact you. Until you find a permanent address as your mail go to the post office general delivery. There is a small fee. After that take, a few days to get to know the island and find a place to live. You might even find time to relax a bit. Any questions?"

"No" replied the four.

"Here are two bags to carry your money. I suggest leaving your money where it is until tomorrow morning. However, feel free to un tape your breasts tonight. Thank you for your time, good luck and God bless you all. goodnight. Oh! And I almost forget. You are free to move about the boat if you want to tonight."

As they exited the captain's quarters, they each exhaled a sigh of relief. They all decided they had each had enough excitement for the day. They were in dreamland within seconds of hitting their bunks.

They were awakened by a bellringing. The big day was here. They were all excited and looking forward to their first day in their new country. The women un taped the money from their bodies and put it in the bags they were given. It felt good. After getting dressed they went to the mess deck.

"Would you folks like some breakfast?" Asked the cook.

"Yes" they replied as they got some coffee.

"We have eggs, toast and bacon" said the cook.

"Sounds good. Thank you." they said.

Cookie gave them their food. "When you finish eating the captain would like you all to join him in his cabin. okay?" She said.

"Okay, thank you." they replied.

After breakfast they were on the way to the captain's cabin when they spotted him standing on the main deck smoking a pipe.

Carefully they approached him "Good morning sir"

"Good morning" replied the captain. "I trust you had a good night's sleep and breakfast?"

"Yes sir" they replied.

"We have a lot to do today so let us get started. We should be done about 4 PM today. Okay?" stated the captain.

"Okay," they replied.

they all left the boat and walked to where the horse-drawn cabs were parked. The view was beautiful streets were cobblestone there were palm trees and flowers. There was a warm breeze. It was a sunny day. It was a tropical paradise. As the five walked to the inauguration office the captain pointed out the open-air restaurant's bakery and many other shops.

"I don't see any cars or trucks." stated John.

"By law only general agencies can have motorized vehicles. It cuts down on air pollution and noise. Most government vehicles are electric only. Only construction machinery and airplanes are gas powered. Only the wealthy can even afford cars or trucks." The captain said as they entered the inauguration building. The four were a little surprised by the revelation the captain had just made. They each decided at that point it was better to listen more and talk less until they understand more about there new home.

The lobby was decorated with plants, waterfalls, and beautiful artwork. All the people were dressed casually.

"Have a seat I'll tell them we are here." As he walked to the desk and asked for a Mr. Mahe. The woman at the desk made a phone call.

"Mr Mahe will be with you shortly," she said.

"Thank ye" replied the captain.

Moments later a black-haired middle-aged man came out and addressed the captain.

The two men shook hands and conversed for a short time. Frank and John and their wives looked at each other with reservation. Finally, the two men addressed the men and their wives.

"Good morning" the man said "I am, Mr. Mahe, the director of inaugurations.

"Good morning" replied the man and their wives.

"If you ladies and gentlemen would come with me will get you or your way to citizenship. There should be an envelope at the desk for you captain and thank you." Mr. Mahe said.

The two couples followed man into a very nicely decorated office with plants, extravagant art, fancy chairs, a mahogany desk, and big windows.

"Won't you folks have a seat please?" he said.

"May I please see your identification?" He asked.

"All we have is our birth certificates." They replied.

"Good enough" he said and took them from the four.

Mr. Mahe picked up the phone and said "Ms. Lee please come to my office and bring some empty neutralization forms with you please. thank you."

Moments later a young extremely attractive woman came in. "Ms. Lee this is Frank, John and their wives. Did you bring the forms with you?" Asked Mr. Mahe.

"Yes sir?" she answered.

"Ms. Lee is going to ask each of you some questions. Please speak clearly and loud enough for her to hear your answer. okay?" Stated Mr. Mahe.

She began with Frank, then John and finished with the women.

"All set." she stated as she handed Mr. Mahe forms.

"Let me see? Frank your surgeon?" He asked.

"Yes sir" Frank replied.

"John you have a doctorate in microbiology?"

"Yes sir." Said John.

"I see you ladies both have college degrees in nursing."

"Yes sir." They replied.

"Subject to passing a physical, Welcome to Zuri." He said smiling.

Both couples were jubilant.

"Ms. Lee please show these folks to the clinic."

"Yes sir."

"Please follow me." she asked the two couples.

At the clinic nurse gave them a medical history form to fill out. After completing the forms, they were seen by the doctor and had blood tests.

The nurse told Ms. Lee she could take them to the indoctrination office.

"Please wait there until they are done with you thank you." Ms. Lee said.

As they walked to the office Frank asked when the physical results would be back.

"If there were problems, we wouldn't be going to the indoctrination office." Ms. Lee answered.

The indoctrination office was a large room with a TV monitor and a few chairs.

"Please take a seat will begin shortly." said the man sitting at the desk.

A few moments later he walked up to them with some papers in his hands.

"I'll need you folks to read and if you agree sign the paper. Your full names please if you have any questions do not hesitate to ask. There are three sections on the paper. Check the appropriate boxes. Before checking the disagree box I suggest you address your concern to me first. Does anybody have any questions currently? If not let us continue. For the next hour you will view a video about our nation. I am sure it will answer some if not all of your questions."

They all watched with great interest. It talked about laws, punishment, benefits, government obligations, citizen obligations, taxes, and schools. After the video, the man asked if there were any questions?

They all raised their hands one by one as he answered all their questions.

"If there were no prisons, how do they deal with serious crime?"

"For a felony we have 30 days hard labor to death depending on the crime and number of times committed. If you take a person's life while committing a crime, it is a mandatory death sentence. If you take what is not yours your household or business is assessed and your fined five times the value of the item, you stole. Half goes to the victim half goes to the government. Repeat offenses get six months hard labor - two years depending on the items value. If you cause injury to another while committing a crime the victim or person of choice can do likewise to you. In all criminal cases the offender's household or business is assessed and the costs of the trial and all expenses or losses to the victim are billed to the defendant. For misdemeanors you may get 48 hours- 30 days chained to the poll of shame in the town square. All costs are billed to your household or business.

All appeals go to the Hall of truth. Their discussion is final. If found guilty, the verdict goes to the punishment board which consists of three persons who serve for 60 days at a time each. Each citizen is required to do their turn except for medical persons. If you are found not guilty no assessment is charged. If a person gives fake testimony knowingly about a defendant, the accuser receives the same punishment the defendant would have received up to and including death.

Our laws are based on the 10 Commandments and the Golden rule taken from the Bible. We have an exceptionally low crime rate. Very rarely do we have repeat offenders."

All four sat there in shock in the laws were terrifyingly strict and left no room for mercy. They began to doubt their choice to leave the United States. However, knowing they had gone too far on their journey to turn back they merely pressed forward.

Another asked about education

"We have the best in the world. Children are required to attend school from age 5 years old until age 18. By the time, a student is 18 years old they can speak English, Latin, and Arabic fluently, as well as read and write the same. They can also learn French or German if they choose or also Italian.

Math and science are a must. Most students have the equivalent of a bachelor's degree by the time they finish school at age 18. We have a wide assortment of trade schools for those wishing to take them. For those that need it we have special education as well as schools for the blind and deaf. Our secondary schools include law, medicine, engineering, dentistry, and many more. The cost is based on household income and the students grade average."

After that, the man said, "Here are manuals explaining the basics of our nation. Medical related persons are given a financial bonus to set up housekeeping. I now need you check the appropriate boxes and sign the papers you were given and hand them to Ms. Lee. Thank you for your attention you may converse amongst yourselves if needed. Not too long please."

After the man left the room they talked for short time as instructed. After Ms. Lee collected the paper she said, "please follow me." And they did. They were taken to what looked like a court room. Please have a seat Ms. Lee said and they did. A few moments later a man came into the room and said "I am justice Merric please rise and raise your right hand and repeat after me."

He began, "please repeat the oath of allegiance and loyalty to the nation after me." When they were done the justice congratulated them and left the room.

Ms. Lee gave each of them a hard copy of the oath. She asked them all to sign it and they did.

"From here you get a government ID. It takes about five minutes. After that we go to the bank and the hotel. After that, your time is yours for the rest of the day. For the next three days I suggest you get to know your new nation and investigate available housing. Also take a few moments to look over the manual given you. The government will cover a 15-day hotel stay as you are all medical staff." Ms. Lee informed them. "you all have four days until you all have to attend a career seminar at the hospital."

Ms. Lee wished them good luck and went on her way.

The desk clerk gave each of them a map of the island and list of restaurants and businesses.

"If you need transportation, let me know so I can arrange it." He gave them their room keys and said "If we can be of service during your stay please don't hesitate to ask." The two couples went to their rooms. The rooms were luxurious and beautiful. It felt so good take a hot shower.

"I saw a clothing store next to the hotel." said John's wife to her husband, "Then perhaps we could go out to lunch."

The phone rang. "Hello," said John. "Frank and I are going clothes shopping and have lunch are you interested in joining us?"

"My wife and I just had the same conversation." replied John. "We will meet you in the lobby in 30 minutes."

"Okay" they both said and hung up.

The men and women split up in the clothing store and met up again by the cashier. The ladies got sundresses and shorts outfits and underwear. The men got casual shirts, pants and shorts and underwear. The sign on the walls said government and medical staff receive a 10% discount on all purchases.

After paying for their purchases they returned to their hotel rooms and changed clothes. It felt good to be in clean fresh clothing. They discarded their old clothing. They went to lunch. They were all very hungry. After lunch they got a cab and toured the island. There was a warm gentle breeze, the scenery was beautiful. It was romantic. After a time, they came on an open-air bar restaurant. John asked the driver if he be willing to wait while they had refreshments. He even asked the driver to join them hoping they could get a local's impression of their new home. The driver stopped the carriage and excepted courteously. As they sat and sipped their drinks, they asked the driver a lot of questions. John asked the driver how long he had been a cabbie. "I have been a cabbie for 50 years." he replied.

"You don't look over 40 years old." said John's wife.

"average age here is 95 years old." he said.

"That is amazing!" Frank exclaimed.

"Are you folks' tourists?"

"No," they replied, "we are new citizens."

"The beach is beautiful" said John's wife. "It certainly is" they all agreed.

"Do we have time to explore it?" John's wife asked the cabbie.

"Of course, sweet thing." he replied.

They all went on the beach. The sand was clean the water was clear blue. They could see the floor. As they walked through the surf, they each marveled at how warm and beautiful it was.

As they watched the sun set the cabbie said, "It time to get you folks our way back to their hotel."

They passed a building with a sign that said dairy processing unit.

"We haven't seen any cows?" they commented.

"There are not any." the cabbie responded.

They were confused. "We don't understand?" they said.

"How long have you been here?" the cabbie asked?

"Today." They all said in unison.

"It will all be explained at the orientation very soon." he replied.

When they got down to the hotel, they thanked the cabbie and paid him a big tip. They asked if he could join them for breakfast in the morning.

"Can do." he replied, "Thank you, you folks have a good evening."

When they asked the desk clerk for their key's he also gave them messages they had received. They thanked the clerk and asked if he could recommend a reliable real estate agent.

"That I can do." the clerk replied, "but being medical staff, your orientation will be taken care of that."

The message read

Be at the hospital at 10 AM, the day after next for orientation and duty assignment.

Breakfast will be served. Transportation will be furnished.

They went into the hotel lounge, ordered a few cocktails, and talked about their day and what they were going to do tomorrow.

They contemplated many things. It seemed as though the island was ran in a military fashion. The security of having permanent employment and knowledge that they would not have to worry about whether they had a roof over their heads and food in their bellies was comforting. However, there was a small part in their mind that wondered was all this too good to be true. After all, if there life in the states had taught them anything it was that government run health care systems could be very dangerous for the patients. And even more dangerous for the doctors and patients that questioned them.

The next day went by quickly but enjoyable.

The next morning, they were awake by a call from the desk clerk. "Coffee is hot and on its way."

by the time they had showered and got dressed the coffee arrived.

The Woman also gave them a message from the desk clerk:

Your cab will be arriving at 9:30 AM. It is raining but do not worry your carriage has a roof.

Frank and his wife came to John and his wife's room. As the two couples drank their coffee, they anticipated how the orientation would go and what it would cover. They all had a lot of questions about a lot of things. At 9:25 AM phone rang.

"Your cab is here." said the voice on the phone.

John replied, "we'll be right down, thank you."

They went to the lobby and outside there was a covered carriage waiting for them. The rain had stopped.

"you want the roof up or down?"

"Down is fine." they replied.

When they arrived at the hospital, they were surprised how big the building was. Upon entering the building, the receptionist sent them into conference room 103. Ms. Lee greeted them with a big smile. "Breakfast will be shortly help yourself to coffee and juice." Ms. Lee gave each one a thin book. "Look over the booklet. Any questions you have will be answered shortly."

After reading the booklet Frank said, "If half of the booklet is true, I am impressed, and frightened at the same time."

They all agreed.

A man came in with a cart of food it smelled delicious.

"Please help yourself and enjoy."

After breakfast a distinguished man, Mr. Mahe, Ms. Lee, and a man in uniform came in. Ms. Lee stood up and said, "we will begin. Going left to right you have met Mr. Mahe, to his right is commander Neal to his right is president Dola. We will watch three short videos. Please pay close attention. Thank you."

The videos were political propaganda fascinating enough to convince even the biggest sceptic that the island was heaven on earth. But the four knew better. They knew there was no such thing as perfect. As Christians themselves they appreciated the biblical based government but wondered if perhaps the countries leaders had missed the whole part in the bible about gods grace and Romans 3:23.

After the videos, Mr. Mahe said Ms. Lee and sat down.

"Good morning it's good to see you all again. I hope all your needs have been met? if not please let me know. I can see you all have questions so let me begin. What I cannot answer one of the other gentlemen can."

The four asked how did you destroy and invasion in four days?

"We greeted them as liberators. Took them into our homes, immobilized them, harvested their usable organs, and used what was left to fuel our electric generators. What equipment we could not use went to scrap. Healthy young females went to the dairy processing plant. Not one citizen lost their life."

All four gulped. The dark side of the island was beginning to rear its head and they began to wonder whether they really meant to give them a job or if they were just pulling their leg before they slaughtered them.

"Our cab driver said he had driven a cab for 50 years he looked 40 years old. Have we found the fountain of youth?" they asked.

"We have technology to transplant every organ in the body except the brain and nerve system. We have cures for all cancers, STDs, Alzheimer's, blindness, loss of hearing and most diseases known to man. The average age of our citizens is 95 years old." They looked forward in awe. "How old do you think Ms. Lee is?" asked Mr. Mahe. All four looked at each other unsure.

"25 years old," said Frank.

"She is 63." answered Mr. Mahe.

"Moving along doctors, nurses, and scientists spend their first three weeks in our trauma center. The scientists go to the most modern lab in the world. Surgeons go to transplant units. Nurses, depending on the training, either go to surgery or trauma care. Because of our life expectancy, permission from the government is required to have a child. The more experience you have the higher the pay. All professional matters are handled by chief surgeon Dr. Mowhee. As medical staff you can buy or rent your choice. The government will pay down payment and closing costs. You must agree to work there for at least 20 years to receive your benefits. Here is the name and address of our real estate office. It is now lunchtime. If you have any more questions do not hesitate to contact my office or Ms. Lee. Meeting adjourned."

Frank, John, and their wives walked out of the hospital amazed and confused.

The cabbie said, "whereto?"

"I think we will walk thank you." replied John. "How about we check out the business district" asked Frank's wife?

"Sounds good to us the weather is beautiful," the others replied.

As they went from one shop to the other, they wondered how old the shopkeepers were. They went into a shop that sold dairy products. Cheese and such. The shopkeeper offered them samples of the different products.

"These are delicious!" they exclaimed.

"Try this." the shopkeeper said and handed them a beverage.

"What is it? And how much is it?"

"It tastes very good."

"It's a dollar 25 per half gallon. It is made of milk and fruit. It is our nation's third largest export." he said.

They bought three kinds of cheese and half gallon of the beverage.

"Refrigeration is required." the shopkeeper said.

They bought homemade bread and pastries next door to the dairy store. They went back to the hotel from there. At the hotel, the clerk gave them a message.

You are invited to visit the president's house for dinner at 7 PM.

"Can I convey your acceptance?" asked the desk clerk.

"Please do." they replied.

They went to their rooms. John's wife called the desk clerk. "Would you have some coffee to sent to the room please?"

"Yes ma'am" he replied," it will be there shortly."

"These pastries looked delicious," said John as he bit into one. "Yum they are try one?" he said to his wife.

She did.

"They are yummy"

The phone rang.

"Hello" said Frank.

"I'm calling from Dr. Mowlee's office. He would like you to report to work Monday at 9 AM."

"We will be there. Thank you for the call." replied Frank.

"Have a good day," the caller said, "good bye."

John got a similar call. There was a knock on the door.

"Your coffee ma'am," and a message.

"Thank you" said John's wife. "John we got a message from the desk clerk.

A cab to be here at 630.

"We'll be ready," said John.

Frank and his wife came into John's room.

As they enjoyed the pastries and beverages, they talked about the day's events.

Dinner with the president was very pleasant it was an outdoor barbecue. Roasted pig, fruits, and a lot of local dishes and wine.

Based on the following days findings and moving into permanent housing. It was a busy time.

Monday was an exciting day for the new comers.

Upon arrival to the hospital they were given their pay statistics and job assignments. They were also given a tour of the organ bank. They were impressed but were afraid to ask whether they were humanly harvested. The hospital had the ability to transplant limbs and all organs except the brain and nerve system. They were given their national response assignments. They were taken to their job assignment stations. The first day was interesting it went by quickly. The three weeks passed quickly. They all saw things and learn things they found to be unbelievable or unheard of before. The doctor and two nurses went to the transplant unit. They were surprised at how many transplants took place every day. The organs and limbs were replaced or used to fire the electric generators. Over a period of a year maybe 150 to 200 people died mostly by accidental causes. Usable organs were harvested. The remains went to the electric generator. When a person dies a place is put in the hall of memories with their name, date of birth, and date of death. The island was small and there was a land shortage.

Everything was good as the months and years came and went. Their reservations slowly melted away as they forgot about their old life. One warm and summery day Dr. Mowlee got appointed chief medical officer of Zuri.

Frank was appointed chief surgeon at the hospital. They both were called up to a top security conference. Mr. Mahe presided over the meeting.

He began, "As you know most of nations of the world have failing economies and their governments that are all but collapsed. The powerful nations are controlling their citizens using cruelty and mass execution. Basically, they are dictatorships. Several the leaders want to come here for medical care and sanctuary. In their own nations if their people are not trying to kill them their government members are. There is an open rebellion in the streets with gun battles between government, police, and the population. We have no jobs openings for dictators. For a fee, their weight in gold or silver we are letting them come here. We will find a purpose for them after screening them for disease. The reason your doctors are at this meeting is you will be dealing with these people directly. Our electric generators will be needing fuel. Tell your staff members to treat them with the utmost dignity and respect until such time as we show them our electric generators."

Frank gulped. He was having a serious moral dilemma. He became a doctor to save lives not to take them. He had committed many sins in his life, but he wondered if outright murder was one, he could live with. After all These men may not have been honorable but to kill them in such a dishonorable way made them just as dishonorable.

"What about their families?" Frank asked. Covering up his skepticism

"They will also see the generators." Dr. Mahe answered.

"We have no need or use for murders or their families, except for a few known dictatorships, the rest of the world is in total chaos. The whole American continent is having a civil war as well as most of Europe, the Middle East and Asia. I'm surprised they haven't used nuclear weapons on each other yet. To restore order in the world nations are paying for a world government. Once nations are now states of the government. Our nation was told to send a representative to the world government meeting in New York. We thanked them for the opportunity and declined their invitation. We told them our nation is a independent nation. We take no position in the world's politics or its problems. We are a peaceful nation with no wish to expand our territory now or anytime in the future. We feel we can be more of a benefit to the nations of the world government by keeping an independent democracy and neutral nation."

Mr. Mahe ended by stating, "Our government expects an invasion from the world government nations. However, there is no need to be concerned. We have developed that technology to destroy invading forces before they are in striking distance of the island. Because of national security I will not elaborate. In the event it should become necessary to inform the public of an invasion, we will do so, otherwise the government will dispose of the invaders without inconveniencing the island population. once the invading forces have been dealt with, we will inform the population. Before destroying an invading force, we will give them every opportunity to withdraw peaceably without harm.

A newspaper lay on the table Frank sat at. The headline read....

AN OUTBREAK OF ARACHIS HYPOGEA

RESEARCHERS INVESTIGATING THE SOURCE.

But before Frank had a chance to read it the meeting was adjourned.

Days weeks and months passed. From time to time there would be a short article in the newspaper that an invasion attempt had taken place and the invading force was destroyed with no loss of life or inconvenience to the island population.

One-time Frank, John, and their wives took a cab ride after an article appeared in the paper looking for the weapons used to repel the invaders. None were ever seen. One day while Frank and John were on the beach, they saw what looked like military ships on the horizon. They thought they should inform the authorities.

Within moments after the ships were seen by them the ships were vaporized. They could not believe their eyes did they really see the ships, or did they imagine what they saw. It was both scary and impressive. They realized their homeland was an advanced and powerful nation to live in.

There was an article in the paper announcing that a lottery will take place in three days to issue permission to have a child. 200 permits will be issued. Families without children get priority. The drawing will be held during our annual Founder's Day three Day celebration. Those winners will have five days to claim their permits. The whole population attended the festival. During the festival, an invading force was seen. everybody watched in awe as they were vaporized in moments.

Everybody cheered! Everybody but john and Johns wife Angel that is. Angel had become pregnant. John and she had kept it a secret in hopes that their name would be in the lottery. But their hopes were dashed when the 200 names were announced, and they were not on the list. Now faced with the choose of either have a forced government abortion or the leaving their new home and raising their child in a war-torn dictatorship. They were once again lost and scared. They did the only thing they knew would help. They went home and prayed. The world they lived in may have been filled with hate, violence, and fear, but They knew that if they trusted God to guide them, they had nothing to fear...

www.ingramcontent.com/pod-product-compliance
Lightning Source LLC
Chambersburg PA
CBHW070944120726
47908CB00005BA/1510